Cotton Candy Sally

Finds a Home

The Sally Horse Chronicles #1

Karen Belove

Walla Walla
County Libraries

Karen Belove
Rhinebeck, New York

The Sally Horse Chronicles #1, Cotton Candy Sally Finds a Home
Copyright © 2016 Karen Belove
Published by Karen Belove in New York

Publisher's Note: This novel is a work of fiction. Cotton Candy Sally was a real horse owned by the author, but the incidents and places are all fictional. All other names, characters, places, and incidents are either products of the author's imagination or used fictitiously. All characters except for Cotton Candy Sally are fictional, and any similarity to people living or dead is purely coincidental.

Dedicated with love and gratitude to Lynda W. of Council Bluffs, Iowa and to the spirit of a beautiful horse named Cotton Candy Sally.

Chapter One

Cotton Candy Sally looked behind her and gave Dutch a stern warning. But that didn't stop the yearling from pulling even harder on her tail. So Sally drew her ears back, threw her head up, and lifted her hind legs in a half-hearted kick. She easily could have made contact, but Sally knew that Dutch was a youngster, and still learning how to properly act in a herd. Besides, he was her friend. She let out a high-pitched squeal and kicked higher, grazing his chest. Dutch took her warning seriously this time, tossed his head, and trotted away in defeat.

She walked over to the fence separating the paddock from the road and nibbled on the sweet new dandelions of early summer. After a few minutes, she looked up and nickered to Hunting Pony. He was across the road in another paddock, but close enough for them to see each other. *"I'm here!"* he answered, then lowered his head back down to the tender blades of grass. He was Sally's favorite. Quiet, unassuming, sweet little Hunting Pony.

Up above, a red hawk soared across a cloudless blue sky, and a light breeze carried the faint smell of lavender through the paddocks. Life was good today for the horses in Council Bluffs, Iowa. But all that was about to change.

***

It happened one Saturday morning in September. Like every other dawn, the night lifted its veil and the farm slowly emerged from darkness. The barn doors rattled open and dogs barked in the distance. The workers went into the stalls and, as they poured a sweet-smelling mixture of oats and pellets into each bucket, the horses nickered softly with pleasure. But Sally was uneasy. She ate her breakfast and kept one ear cocked. The men were moving too quickly, and they were tense.

Every morning after breakfast, Lico, Jan, and Francis – the men who worked at the barn – put halters on the horses and took them out of their stalls, carefully looking them over. Then they led the horses, one by one, down the dirt path and out to the pastures. Sally had five pasture mates and she knew them very well. After all, she shared the same field with them for eight years, ever since she was a foal. Before that, she was turned out only with her mother, in the big broodmare paddock next door. Sally was born here at the farm and, except for when she went to a horse show, she knew no place else. Her home was and always had been at Gone Away Farm, here in the peaceful Iowa country.

But on this September morning, nobody came to get the 15.3 hand quarter horse. Some of the horses — like Dutch and another young horse named Comet – were impatient and started to kick the walls. They wanted to go out and any change in their routine made them edgy.

It was 9:00 when Lico finally took Sally out and put her on cross ties. But instead of bringing her out to the field, he put shipping boots on her legs. Dutch and Hunting Pony were already on cross ties, their boots on and fastened. Sally stood in the aisle attached to the ropes and watched as the men took all the other horses out of their stalls and put boots on them, too.

Just then, Lauren – the barn owner – walked out of the tack room and down the aisle.

"Jose, what's your problem?" she yelled. "If you moved any slower you'd be standing still!"

Now she turned to Jan. "All those saddles are supposed to go, too. Where are they, and why aren't they ready?" Her voice was shrill and unsteady. She said loudly, "I thought I made it very clear to everyone what needed to be done, and when!"

Then, right in the middle of the aisle, she started to cry. She just stopped in her tracks, dropped her head in her hands, and started sobbing. Lauren never yelled around the barn, and Sally had never, ever seen her cry.

This bothered the mare so much that she shuffled on the cross ties and tried to break free. If she could just get off the ropes and into the pasture, she thought everything would be okay. Dutch kicked the tack trunk in the aisle and tried desperately to lift his front end off the ground, but the ropes kept bringing him back down. That got Solomon, the big bay horse from Canada, so upset that he started whinnying and pawing the ground with his front foot.

"HEY!" yelled Lauren, sniffling. She was mad, and

hollered, *"HEY! Cut it out, now!"* Then she started to cry again.

She walked over to Sally and said, "I'm sorry, girl. I'm so sorry…"

She wrapped her arms around Sally's neck and burrowed her face deep into the soft hairs of Sally's coat. Sally rested her head on Lauren's shoulder. They stayed like that for a long time, and Lauren's tears made Sally's shoulder wet and salty.

"We've come so far together," Lauren said as she ran her hands over Sally's neck. "You and me. So many blue ribbons. So many perfect hunter shows. You jump your fences in stride, every time… everybody knows Gone Away Farm because they all know *you*…"

And everything she said was true. People in Council Bluffs liked to say that Sally had beautiful eyes — not only in how she sized up a fence, but also because they were just… so pretty. Big, deep, dark eyes that seemed to say *"I understand, I'm confident, I'll take care of you."*

Lauren whispered to Sally, "You've always been my favorite. But there's nothing I can do…"

"A divorce is bad enough," she sobbed. "But to have to give up the farm. My life. My horses. It's just unbearable."

Lauren's brother Jake walked up to them, put his arm around Lauren's shoulder, and gently pulled her away.

"Come on, Lauren," he said softly. "They're waiting. We need to put them on the trailer."

Sally stood like a soldier, staring at the two of them. With a feeling of uncertainty and foreboding, she watched them walk away.

***

When the horses traveled to shows, Lauren loaded them onto a trailer, but today strangers did the job. Their names were Dan and Roy, and they were all business.

They loaded horse after horse onto a big rig. Some, like Solomon and Hunting Pony, walked right up the ramp, turned effortlessly once inside, and backed into the straight stall behind them. Other horses without much experience, like Dutch, were afraid. When Dan tried to lead him on, Dutch threw his hind end to the right and then the left – anything rather than walk up that vertical incline. Finally, running with him so that Dutch was up the ramp before the horse even knew it, Dan turned him, backed him up, and tied him in his stall.

Now it was Sally's turn. Dan snapped the lead line to her halter and she walked obediently after him. But she didn't like the ramp – it was steeper than it had looked from far away. So when it came time to load, she swung her hind end to the left, threw her head up high, and tried to get loose. She just wanted to go out to the paddock, but Dan wasn't having any part of that. He led her in a circle, pulled hard on the lead line, and tried again. This time, Sally swung her body to the right.

Then she sensed someone approaching from behind.

"Stupid horse, I don't have time for this!" Roy growled, and before she knew it, he whipped her hard, right across her flank.

It hurt, so she kicked out and he whipped her again. Then she lifted her front feet off the ground, and twisted in mid-air, almost lifting Dan off the ground.

"Hey man, stop, STOP!" Dan yelled. "You're just making it worse. She'll kill us both!"

Before she even knew what was happening, Dan quickly turned her in a circle, and ran her right up the ramp, like he did with Dutch. He turned her around, backed her up, and tied her into her stall, right next to

Chapter Two

For hours, they drove at a steady 50 mph pace; it was a monotonous, long drive that never seemed to end. The horses were tired from standing for so long in one position, constantly having to shift their weight to balance themselves around the turns and undulations of the road. The only time they had a break was for five or six hours when the rig stopped overnight at a motel. That's when the horses slept.

Dan was nice to the horses, and when they stopped for a trailer check, he gave them a pat and told them they'd be okay. But Roy was rough, and when he cleaned the manure out of the stalls, he hit the horses if they didn't move out of the way fast enough. They were afraid of him — especially Dutch, who backed his head away whenever Roy raised his hand to the horse. The fun-loving and playful Dutch that Sally knew and loved, the one that pulled on the horses' tails and tugged on their blankets, was gone now. This Dutch was quiet and subdued, and tried to get as close to the other horses as possible. The trip was hard for all of them, and it showed in their tired faces and the weary way they carried themselves.

Finally, after two full days of driving, they passed a sign that said, "Welcome to New Jersey." They traveled for another half hour until the rig pulled into a driveway and stopped in a large parking lot with horse trailers of all sizes and shapes. The men disappeared for a few minutes and then approached the side of the rig, unhooked the lock, and opened the door. They pulled down the ramp and the horses came to attention as the cold air rushed in to greet them.

The horses had arrived. *Jersey Livestock, horse auction.* One thousand sixty-one miles, and a whole world away from Council Bluffs.

Even before they were out of the trailer, the horses got nervous and shuffled in place. It was because of the smell. The odor of horses mixed in with faint gas fumes and old bedding. It was a scent that was oddly familiar, but not quite right.

Dan and Roy led the horses off the trailer and into a big building with wooden corrals. They split up the load and divided the horses into two side-by-side enclosures. There were fourteen horses in total from Iowa, and seven went in each corral.

The enclosures were small, though, only big enough for five horses, so it was way too close for comfort, even among friends. But the horses were uncertain and insecure, so they let the men push and prod and crowd them in.

Sally was cautious and on edge, and she was covered with a thin film of sweat that came from a bad case of nerves. Hunting Pony, Solomon, Comet, and Dutch were scared, too. Once settled in their paddock, the group stood together in one corner, with the other Iowa horses in the adjoining paddock huddled right next to them — with only the fencing between them.

The whole warehouse was full of corrals that contained more horses of all shapes and sizes. Quarter horses, draft horses, thoroughbreds, all kinds of crossbreds, palominos, bay horses, chestnuts, and paints. Mares and geldings, big and small, passive and aggressive, they were all housed together. Some had shiny coats, pretty manes, and long tails. But others were sick and injured, and they stood lonely in their paddocks, with their heads hung low.

Roy nodded towards the Iowa horses. "These will fetch some good money," he said.

"Yup," Dan replied. He pointed to Sally and said, "This one's young and fit, and very pretty."

A third man chimed in. "Not so sure about that one, though," and he pointed to Hunting Pony. "I think pretty ugly is more like it." And they laughed.

Sally snorted, and pawed at the ground.

Roy said, "Mosaler the wholesaler's coming to take a look. He has his rig, so he'll leave tonight with anything he thinks he can sell right away. The others go on the auction block."

"After that, it's anyone's guess where they end up," Dan said. "Lucky for them if they can leave before the auction starts. All that parading around to the highest bidder — it's rough on a horse."

"I think I hear you getting soft," laughed Roy. "After all this time, you still love the horses – even the old nags and the uglies," he said.

Dan ignored the chiding. He did love the horses, all of them, and he hated when Roy was rough with them. But he didn't argue because he knew better. He knew you couldn't convince someone to understand horses. It was either in your blood, or it wasn't.

"Here comes Mosaler," he said.

Bill Mosaler was tall and muscular, and he walked with purpose, like a man conducting business and getting things done. The skin on his face was rough, as sometimes happens with people who spend a lot of time outdoors. But he had a friendly eye and a generous smile.

He greeted the men. "Hey boys," he said and nodded towards the Iowa horses. "These from Lauren Brady?"

"Yup, just rolled in," Dan replied.

"Hmmm, I'll take a look," Mosaler said as he made his way through the horses and walked over to Sally.

"Whoa girl," he said gently.

Mosaler held onto her halter and shooed the other horses away. Sally put her ears back and tried to jerk her head out of his hand. But he held firm and she stopped.

"It's okay," he said. "I'm not going to hurt you."

"She's a looker," he said to the men. "Is this the 8-year old quarter horse Lauren told me about?"

"Yeah, that's her," said Roy. "But watch that hind

end. She'll kick you if she gets the chance."

Mosaler held Sally's halter and ran his hand down her neck. Sally didn't trust him, but she didn't move, either. She stood like a statue, and if he tried anything, anything threatening or surprising, she was ready to bolt.

He clipped a lead line to her halter, held it in his hand, and bent down to feel her legs. He liked what he saw.

"Okay boys, let's see what she's got," he exclaimed.

He removed the lead line and replaced it with a lounge line. Pulling her behind him, he tried to leave the corral and make his way to the small riding ring across the floor. But Sally went up on her hind legs and snorted; she wasn't about to leave her friends. Solomon and Hunting Pony whinnied to her, Dutch started kicking the fence, and Comet went up in the air.

Mosaler kept Sally to the far end of the corral. "Okay, okay," he whispered.

He turned to face her and muttered under his breath, "You're opinionated, I see that. Just don't push me too far."

Dan walked in to help, and calmed the other Iowa horses. Once everything was quiet, Mosaler tried again to lead Sally to the gate.

"Shhhh," he said. *"Come on girl..."*

She pulled back on the line once, he loosened it, and then she gave up and followed.

As she walked across the dirt floor to the riding ring, Hunting Pony let out a mournful cry behind her. Sally whinnied back to him. *"I'm still here!"* she said.

Once in the ring, Mosaler walked Sally to the far end, stood her up, kept the line loose, and walked about fifteen feet into the center. Then he picked up the line and said, "Okay girl, walk."

Sally was used to working on the lunge line in Iowa, so she knew to walk in a wide circle around Mosaler. "So far so good," he said to the men. Then he turned to face Sally again and said, "Now trot."

She picked up an easy trot. It felt good to move around after being cooped up for so long. She swung her head a few times but kept a steady rhythm and cadence as Mosaler held onto the line. She traveled around him three times in a circle.

"Whoa now," he said. He walked over to her, turned her to face the other direction, and walked into the center again.

Dan and Roy had come along to look. They leaned

over the fence and saw Sally's long stride, and beautiful, spirited trot. A few other people came over to watch as well.

"Pretty mover," said a newcomer. "I guess she won't be going on the block."

"Don't think so," said Roy. "Not sure about the others through. Some will go to a riding school, some to other buyers, some to a re-seller. But some won't get any takers, and once they go for auction – who knows."

"Okay," Mosaler said to Dan. "I've seen enough. Put her back in the corral and meet me in the office. We'll complete the paperwork and I'll move her out tonight."

When they brought Sally back into the corral, the horses cried out to greet her. Sally trotted over to them, then turned to watch the men. She nuzzled Hunting Pony's nose, Dutch lay his head on Sally's back, and Comet rubbed her tail. Big Solomon stood with his head up tall and kept an eye on the whole room; he was protecting his herd. The horses hugged the fence they shared with the other Iowa horses, and the two groups stood close together in this strange new place.

***

At 6:00 pm, carrying a lead line in one hand and paperwork in the other, Mosaler entered the corral and walked over to Sally. He growled at the other horses to move away. Sally moved with them, determined not to be separated from her group again. Mosaler stretched out his arm and grabbed her halter.

"Okay Ms. Opinionated, you're coming with me now, so don't get any ideas."

Sally stood firm and planted her feet on the ground as he tried to lead her out of the enclosure.

"I've had a long day, so don't start with me..." he said firmly.

Sally whinnied and jerked her head up and away.

"Look mare," he said sternly. "I like you well enough, but you're not going to win. You're coming with me whether you like it or not."

Sally didn't want to go, but she was smart; she knew she wasn't going to win a battle with this man. He was nice now, but she knew he would be mean if he felt he had to be.

So when Mosaler pulled the rope behind him, Sally slowly followed, her head hung low and her eyes half closed. As he opened the gate and pulled her out of the corral, she stopped abruptly on the other side, lifted her head high and whinnied so loud and sadly that the sound of her voice echoed through the building.

Hunting Pony tried to follow her, but Mosaler closed the gate before he could make it through. Trapped, he kicked the gate with his leg, lifted his head and called out to his best friend. Sally cried as she was led away, walking behind Mosaler, past the other Iowa horses, through the corrals, and out the door.

As she followed Mosaler into the cold September night, the cries from Hunting Pony, Dutch, and Comet filled the air. As she walked further away from the building and closer to the rig, their sounds faded into the darkness, until she couldn't hear them anymore.

This was the part that Mosaler hated the most. The separation. He had bought and sold horses for over twenty years, yet separating them still broke his heart. But he wouldn't dwell on it. He couldn't. He still had a lot to get done.

Mosaler led Sally up the ramp to his rig, and she stood in a trailer for the second time that day. "Hold tight, mare," he told her. Then he ran down the ramp and left her.

Just as she was about to kick the stall, she smelled

something familiar and stood tall, reaching her head high to get a better scent. *Solomon!* She heard Solomon's footsteps and smelled her friend as he approached the trailer. She let out a tremendous whinny and he answered, *"I'm here, I'm here."*

Sally nickered with joy when she saw him being led up the ramp and onto the trailer to join her. But he had a big gash on his head and there was blood. As Roy maneuvered him into the stall next to Sally, the two horses rubbed each other and blew into each other's face.

"He's a big one, this guy is," said Roy. "But I gave him what for. Let him try to rear up on me again and I'll tell him a thing or two he won't easily forget."

"That's not the way to do it, Roy. You should know that by now. They're just scared," Mosaler said.

Roy shrugged. "Hey – I let them know who's boss, and that's what they respect."

"A horse like that could kill you with one kick if he wanted to, and you know it. I've seen it happen. So if I were you, I'd think twice before beating on him again."

Roy replied, "Yeah, sure, whatever. Well, you're on your own now Mo, so have fun. They're all yours."

And with that, he walked down the ramp, waved good-bye, and told Mosaler he'd see him next time.

Mosaler walked back up the ramp and checked the horses. Solomon would be okay; the gash was only on the surface. But it was an unnecessary thing to do, and Mosaler cursed under his breath.

"Okay guys," he mumbled to the horses, "Here we go!"

With that, Mosaler walked out of the trailer, shut the ramp, fastened the bolts, climbed into the rig, and started the engine. Next stop: New York City. In one hour they would arrive at Bernadette's Riding School, a place about as far away from Council Bluffs as you can get.

Chapter Three

The trip from New Jersey to New York City was full of traffic, noise, and short stops. They traveled a very busy highway, and a few times Mosaler had to put the breaks on so suddenly that Sally and Solomon hit the sides of their stalls hard. But eventually, they arrived. The rig stopped and they heard Mosaler climb out and slam the door. He disappeared for awhile, and when he returned, he opened the ramp and fresh night air filled the trailer. Sally and Solomon stood very still.

Solomon was the first one they took off the rig, and Sally didn't want to be without him. But within minutes, Mosaler was back. He unclipped her halter from the stall, led her down the ramp and out into the night. Once she was on level ground, he let her drop her head to investigate whatever little grass was on the ground. She nibbled on some straggly weeds and heard people approaching.

"This is Cotton Candy Sally," Mosaler said to the group. "The fancy quarter horse hunter, born and bred in the pastures of Iowa."

A pretty woman about 35 years old, dressed in a riding jacket and riding boots, approached slowly, and gently put her hand on Sally's neck.

"Hi Sally," Bernadette said. "Welcome to my riding school."

Bernadette took the lead line out of Mailer's hands and led Sally into a small barn that was right off the pavement, just a short walk from where Mosaler had parked the rig. The barn had all the sweet, familiar scents of home: hay and horse feed mingled in with faint leather smells from all the saddles and bridles and leather cleaners. Bernadette held onto the lead line and walked next to Sally, pulling on the line softly until they reached the back of the barn, where she was led right into a stall. But it wasn't a big box stall that Sally was used to. It was a straight stall – a space only about five feet wide and nine feet long.

Bernadette walked her in, and at the far end of the stall she tied a chain to Sally's halter so that she stood with her face to the wall. There were water and feed buckets that she could easily reach, and she was able to put her head down far enough to eat the hay that was plumped up for her on the floor, but she wasn't free to move her head more than four feet in any direction. It was like being in the trailer, but with no motion of the rig and the road. She tried to bring her head up to look around, but the chain jerked her to a stop. She drank some water and ate her hay. Solomon was in a box stall next to her, so it could have been worse – at least her friend was nearby. The straight stall was a problem because she couldn't lie down, but she was very, very tired. Solomon nickered to her and soon, she fell asleep standing up.

***

The next few weeks at Bernadette's riding school were tough for Sally. In the early mornings, things were a lot like Iowa. The light filtered in through the barn windows as the sun rose, and the horses moved restlessly in their stalls in anticipation of breakfast. Some pawed the ground, some kicked the walls. When Sally and Solomon heard the workers and smelled the sweetness of the feed and hay, they joined in and whinnied to let everyone know they were there and ready to eat.

But after breakfast, the similarities stopped. There was no going outside. There was no turnout, no paddocks, no fields. Instead, the horses stayed in their stalls and ate hay until there was no more hay to eat. That's how it was with horse barns in New York City; pavement instead of pastures.

The barn workers would take the horses out to the cross ties, clean their stalls, then put them right back in. Some of the horses had owners who would visit them, clean them, tack them, and then go outside to ride. But Sally and Solomon were there to become school horses, so they didn't have owners to give them special treatment.

At first, Sally whinnied all the time to go out into the fresh air, to nibble on grass, to stretch her legs and her back. She wanted to run and expel some energy, and walk around a paddock with her friends. But those times never came.

Bernadette was nice, though. She came into Sally's stall every morning and talked to her. Most days, she took her out to the cross ties and curried her, then brushed her and put conditioner in her tail to get all the knots out.

Cleaning her was one thing, but it turned out that riding the bay mare in New York City was something else entirely. When Bernadette tacked her up and led her out into the fresh air, the world was full of cars and trucks, not fields and trails like Iowa. They would walk one block down Pleasant Avenue, turn right onto Lark Street, and then... there was a very busy street called the Clearview Expressway. Sally learned to deal with the neighborhood streets and the cars, but that expressway was a whole different story.

Bernadette was a good rider; she knew how to keep her seat deep down in the saddle with her legs long and firm against Sally's side. But still, did Bernadette really expect her to cross that busy road? The cars and trucks whizzed by so fast that Sally could barely keep her eyes on them, and the noise was almost as frightening as all the movement. Sally had never seen traffic like this before, so her fright and flight instinct took over immediately. That's why the first time they came close to the Expressway, she stopped short, wheeled around, and ran back toward the farm so fast that Bernadette almost fell off.

"Whoa, whoa girl!" Bernadette cried. *"Hold up!"*

Sally went up in the air, twisted around, and tried

her hardest to get back to the barn, but Bernadette held the reins tightly — and turned her back around to face the road. They stood still for a few seconds, facing the expressway, and Bernadette urged her forward, tapping Sally on the flank with a crop. "We're crossing whether you like it or not Ms. Sally!" she said.

Sally was petrified! But Bernadette was quick with her aids and so firm that soon, they were across the busy road before Sally even knew it. Once on the other side, they entered Forest Hill Park and rode the trails. There, on the other side of the road, it was quiet and peaceful – with trails and fields that Sally understood. But crossing that road wasn't worth it.

**

Some of the more experienced riders at the barn tried to take Sally out to the park, too. But they weren't always as nice to her as Bernadette was. To keep her moving forward, most of them hit her hard, over and over again with the crop, and growled at her even before she got to the expressway. She became more and more confused and wondered, *"What do they expect of me... and why are they so angry?"*

Soon, she learned that going outside simply meant

she would get hit and yelled at. So her buck got bigger and bigger each time they took her out — and she would spin around so fast that most riders fell off right onto the street. After awhile, they just didn't try anymore.

Instead, they started riding her in the indoor ring. But Sally had so much pent-up energy that it was hard for her to stay calm. So she started rearing up and bucking even in the ring, and soon everybody was just plain afraid of her. Nobody wanted to ride her anymore. And then, nobody wanted to clean her anymore, either. So she spent more and more time alone in her stall, facing the wall.

Solomon, on the other hand, was happy. He didn't buck or get scared, so the riders liked him — and the more they liked him, the more attention he got. They even took him out to graze on what little grass grew up around the barn. Because he was so good, Bernadette used him as a school horse in the lesson program, so everyone got to know him, and the girls would argue over who got to ride him. They even took him into the indoor ring sometimes without a saddle or rider and let him run free.

Chapter Four

Four times a year, a new class started at the riding school. Whenever school began, there was a lot of buzz in the barn, with new faces mixed in among the regulars. Each class always started the same – Bernadette would put the horses on cross ties, and teach the students how to brush and curry, pick out the horse's feet, and comb their tails. They would start with Solomon, or one of the other horses that were easy to handle. Lastly, Bernadette would take Sally out, and would tell the students how careful they needed to be around a horses' hind end.

Sally rarely got out of her stall these days, and never knew what to expect when she was on cross ties. *Would they take her outside? Would she get hit?* So she stood on the aisle with her ears back, expecting the worst.

"You all saw how easy it was to brush a nice horse," Bernadette would say. "But this is Sally. A horse like her you have to be careful around."

A pretty girl named Lacey said, "Why Bernadette? What does she do?"

"She'll buck and kick you if you don't watch out. She's just an ornery kind of horse," Bernadette answered.

"Why is she so mean?" Lacey asked.

"Some horses are just like that..." Bernadette answered.

"She's very pretty," commented another rider named Lizbeth. "Can we ride her one day?"

"Oh, no, NO!" laughed Bernadette. "I'm the only one who rides Sally because, well, she just doesn't seem to get along with anyone else."

"Watch her ears!" another rider named Jessica said. "When they go back, that means you should run for cover. She bites, too!"

Samantha, one of the regular riders who had joined the group, chimed in. "She's nasty! She wheels up in the air and she bucks people off right before the expressway!"

Bernadette replied, "She's not nasty. And it's

important that you all know that. Sally is just… Sally. She came here all the way from Iowa, and I'm not so sure she likes city life very much."

The girls started talking about all the other horses who did like the city, and how much fun they were.

"Maybe one day, when you girls get to know horses a little bit better, you'll help me figure out how to tame her," Bernadette said, and laughed.

Sally was getting restless on the cross ties and began to paw at the floor.

"Okay," Bernadette told the group," Does anyone want to help me curry and brush her?"

There were no takers. Nobody wanted to touch the mean horse.

Bernadette picked up a curry and, starting at Sally's neck, explained to the group exactly what she was doing, and why. It felt good to Sally, like a massage, so she stood still, and then dropped her neck. Bernadette explained that this meant Sally was relaxing.

After a few minutes, a little girl in work boots picked up a brush and asked quietly if she could help.

"Of course, Kara, that would be great," Bernadette replied. "And since you'll be working with me, I think this is a fine way to start."

As Bernadette brushed one side of her, Kara brushed the other. Sally's eyes closed and she looked like she would fall asleep.

Everybody was so focused on Bernadette and Kara brushing the horse that nobody noticed Annie, a new rider to the group, had picked up a comb and grabbed Sally's tail. "She's not so bad, I'm going to help!"

Annie yanked on Sally's tail and pulled hard, trying to get the tangles out.

It all happened very fast. Sally was startled and put her ears back before Bernadette could tell Annie to step away. Sally swiftly lifted her right hind leg as a warning. One of the girls screamed, and Bernadette firmly announced there was no yelling in a barn, ever. But Sally lifted her leg again, and kicked out, and Annie jumped out of the way just in time to avoid contact.

Bernadette yelled at Sally and slapped her in the ribs. *"Sally, NO!"*

"Oh my God," someone said, "She is *so nasty!*"

"No wonder nobody pays her any attention."

"Sally's a bully!"

"Sally's a donkey!"

"Sally's a pig!"

Sally didn't really know what was going on, but she knew it wasn't good. So she stood there, waiting for something else bad to happen.

Bernadette told the girls to go into the tack room. When they were gone, Bernadette took her off the cross ties.

"Sally, really? Why do you do these things?" Bernadette said. "If you can't adjust, you're going to have to go down the road, and who knows what will happen to you. Can't you just be good... once in a while?"

Sally nuzzled Bernadette's hand. "I love you, girl, but I give up," Bernadette told her. "I can't have a horse here that no one can ride, and who's a danger to the kids." With that, she put Sally back in her stall and clipped her halter to the chain.

Chapter Five

It was getting dark out, and most of the girls had gone home. The workers were cleaning the barn, feeding and giving water, and then last of all, they threw hay into the stalls for the horses. It was quiet and Sally listened to the soft sound of happy horses, eating their hay and drinking their water.

"Hi, girl," Kara to her said softly.

She was standing at the opening of the stall, on the right side of Sally's hind end. "Can I come in, or are you going to kick me, too?"

The chain had just enough give for Sally to turn her head and see Kara standing there. She put her ears back and thought, *"leave me alone!"*

"I'm not going to hurt you, Sally. I think you're kind of cute."

Sally kept her ears back, almost flat on her head now. One more step and she'd kick.

"Okay, okay, I'll go. But one day I'm going to ride you, Sally. I will. Because I know how to be nice to a horse. And I know how to ride."

Bernadette was sweeping the aisle, watching them.

"Don't get your hopes up with her," Bernadette said. "I'm afraid Sally's damaged goods. And I don't know how long we can keep her here if she's not going to earn her keep."

"Besides," Bernadette said, "I have a lot of other things to keep you busy. How about grabbing a broom, and helping me sweep up?"

"Sure," Kara replied.

"Kara," Bernadette said. "Your mother told me you used to ride horses at your grandparent's house on Long Island. Is that true?"

"Yes," she said. "We all lived there on the farm — my mom, my dad and me. My dad worked the farm with Grandpa, and I helped take care of the horses."

"That sounds great," Bernadette said, hoping Kara might tell her more. She kept sweeping as she turned the corner down the next aisle. Kara followed her.

There was a moment of silence before Kara added,

"Of course, that all changed when my dad got sick. They sold the farm because my Grandpa couldn't do it all by himself."

"I'm sorry about that Kara," Bernadette replied softly.

They swept the barn without talking. It was very quiet except for the sounds of the horses eating their grain and munching on hay. To Kara, these were some of the most beautiful sounds in the world. Everything was so quiet and peaceful, and the horses always seemed happy when they were eating. Even the smells were wonderful; the aroma of the oats and the pellets mixed in with sweet feed and hay. At Bernadette's, there were always a few cats around too, to keep the mice away. They had just eaten their dinner, so two of them – Huey and Dewey – were being lazy on a tack trunk, licking their lips. Kara could have stayed all evening. It reminded her of the days when she helped on her grandfather's farm. The good days.

Suddenly, out of nowhere, Kara said, "He died, you know. My dad."

"Yes honey," Bernadette said. "Your mom told me..."

Kara wanted to tell Bernadette how much fun she

had with her dad – how funny he was, and about all the things he had taught her about horses. She wanted to explain how much she missed him, and how life just wasn't the same anymore. But she didn't know where to start.

So they swept the barn in silence until Kara's mother finally arrived to take her home.

Chapter Six

Kara worked at the barn two days a week after school, and half days both Saturday and Sunday. Her mom didn't have a lot of money after her father died, so she couldn't simply ride and play with the horses like the other girls. Instead, she worked at the barn in exchange for riding and taking lessons from Bernadette.

She had to clean everybody else's tack, haul hay from the hay loft, pick out the manure from the horse's stalls, and each day she had to scrub the tack room clean. But she was okay with the work, because when no one was around, she saw all the little things that made the barn so special. The cats for example. They hunted night and day, and never let a mouse get into the feed bins. They weren't very friendly when the barn was busy, but if it was quiet, they would let Kara pet them, and they'd curl up in her lap. There was a dog there too, named Weasel. Weasel was smart about horses and knew to avoid their feet so that he wouldn't get stepped on. But the best was, of course, the horses. They all had their own personalities and quirky behaviors.

After a few weeks, Bernadette let her help feed the horses too, and throw them their hay. Kara loved feeding, because she could go into all the horse's stalls, and talk to them. Even Sally got used to her and stopped pinning her ears back or threatening to kick when Kara approached. After all her chores were done and the horses were fed, she loved to give her special horses carrots and sugar cubes that Bernadette kept tucked away in the tack room.

Kara loved the animals, but she didn't care for the girls at the barn. She just felt… out of place. While she didn't have money to spend on horse clothes and tack, they had fancy saddle pads and would *ooh and ahh* every time someone showed up in a new pair of boots or britches. And whenever Kara tried to tell them about the personalities of the cats, or the funny things some of the horses did when the barn was quiet, they just changed the subject. All of the things that Kara loved most, they didn't seem to care about.

But there was another thing, too. They all had mothers *and* fathers. They didn't know what it was like to lose everything – your house, your barn, *your family.* They didn't understand what it was like to be… Kara.

One day when she was cleaning the tack room, she heard the girls talking in the aisle.

Samantha whispered, "So, I heard that Kara works here because she doesn't have any money. I think she's poor."

"That's *so sad,*" replied Lacey. "But what's worse is… I don't think she even knows how to ride!"

Soon Lizbeth joined in. "I think you're right! Did you notice she never gets on a horse when we're here?"

"She's probably embarrassed to ride in front of us…" Jessica snickered.

Then Annie chimed in. "And why does she always hang around that Sally horse? Maybe they're two peas in a pod!"

"So strange."

"It's weird."

"They're weird…"

"… And you know what else? I heard that her father is dead."

Then, everyone started talking at once.

"Oh my *God!*"

"Well, that explains things…."

"Poor Kara…"

Kara hid in the tack room until they got on their horses and went into the ring to ride.

Then she started to cry.

"They are so mean!" she thought.

Life was just unfair. Her father was a better horseman than all of them put together. And she used to have lots of horses – not just one, like them. Suddenly, she didn't like being at the barn anymore. Maybe she would tell Bernadette she had to quit, that she just wasn't into riding and the horses anymore.

But later that day, as she fed the horses their dinner, she changed her mind. The horses nickered and nudged her as she filled the buckets with grain, and again — the sweet smells of the feed and the hay made her feel good. She liked the horses. No, she *loved* the horses.

That evening when she went into Sally's stall to feed her, she put her arms around Sally's neck, rested her head against Sally's shoulder and cried. "Oh Sally, I just want my father back… I want things to be the way they used to be. Nothing is ever going to be the same." Her tears were making Sally's coat all wet, but she didn't care.

After a very long time, she stepped back and realized what she had done. She had walked into nasty Sally's stall and easily could have been kicked or bitten. But the mare had not once put her ears back, or lifted her leg to kick. Instead, she gave Kara a nudge on her shoulder. Kara looked right into the mare's eyes, and then petted her face. "I love you, Sally," she said. "You're very, very special…"

Then she did something that she knew would have made Bernadette very mad. She unhooked Sally's chain and let the horse rub on her, and check her pockets for treats. "One day, Sally, I'm going to ride you, just like Bernadette does. You and me."

What she didn't realize was that Bernadette was watching her from down the aisle the whole time. And her heart ached for both of them.

***

Sally liked Kara. At first, she could care less about the little girl who worked at the barn. But the more time she spent around Kara, the more she trusted her. Of course, Kara would pet her, and give her treats. But it was more than that. She was gentle, and there was something deep down inside of that girl Sally felt comfortable with. Confident with. She liked when Kara was around, and after a few weeks, she would nicker whenever she heard Kara's footsteps in the barn.

It was on a Thursday afternoon, the week after Kara overheard the girls talking, when everything changed.

Bernadette met her as she walked into the barn. "I need you to help me with something," she said. "We need Sally to earn her keep if she's going to stay here."

"Anything!" Kara said.

"Good, because you're going to ride her today."

Kara almost lost her breath. Was this really happening? She loved Sally and wanted more than anything to get on her back and ride, but what if it didn't work out? She knew enough about horses to realize that a bond on the ground didn't necessarily mean the horse wouldn't buck you off. And Sally was getting worse and worse. Bernadette was so busy at the barn that she hardly had time to ride Sally anymore. And the less she was ridden, the more difficult she was under tack.

"You're a good rider, Kara. You're now doing things

in our lessons that make me think you can do this. But remember, just because the horse likes you doesn't mean you can ride her."

"I know," Kara said.

"Are you scared?"

"I'm not scared of falling off. I just want it to work. If it doesn't, I know what that means for Sally."

"Okay then. We're going to do this the right way," Bernadette said. "First, we're going to lunge her, which will make her a little tired, and help calm her down. Then, you're going to focus on riding correctly to make this easy for Sally."

"Okay," Kara said definitively. "I can do this!"

But inside, she was a bundle of nerves.

Bernadette went into the tack room to do some chores, and Kara walked with purpose into Sally's stall. "Okay girl," she said. "Be nice to me, please!" Sally nickered to her.

She took Sally out of the stall and put her on the cross ties. Kara curried her until her coat shined, and brushed out her tail so that it was long and flowing. Then she put the saddle on. Sally stood like a soldier, she never pawed the ground or put her ears back once. She looked so beautiful! Kara left the halter on and met

Bernadette in the riding ring.

Bernadette attached a lunge line to Sally's halter and told the horse to trot. Sally tried to tug her head away from the line, but then trotted as she was told. "Good girl," Bernadette said, "Good girl…"

But when Bernadette told her to canter, Sally threw her head up high, ran at full speed, and kicked out at the same time. She was full of energy, and she was going to let them both know it. She was thinking, *"Let me off this line and let me run free!"*

Bernadette held the lunge firmly in her hand, leaning back so that the weight of her body braced against Sally's pulling of the line. "Easy, easy," she said over and over again. "Easy Sally…"

Kara stood still and her face went white. This was not a good sign.

Bernadette kept the line tight and never took her eyes off the horse, but she knew that Kara was scared. She laughed and said, "Stop worrying, Kara! She's fine. She's being a horse! She'll calm down, believe me. Better she gets her energy out now than when you're on her back!"

"Trot," Bernadette said. "Now canter."

This went on for another twenty minutes, until

finally, Sally cantered with her head down, nice and easy. Kara thought she looked like a show horse, so pretty and fluid.

"Okay," Bernadette said. "Your turn. Get on..."

Bernadette met her at the mounting block, and Kara put the bridle on. She petted Sally on the neck.

"Don't choke her, she hates that. And keep your heels down," Bernadette said.

Sally let Kara climb on and take the reins, then they walked to the side of the ring. Kara could feel her tense up, so she put her heels down as low as they could get, and gave the horse a little nudge with her leg.

"Good," said Bernadette. "Keep walking, and when you're ready, go ahead and trot."

The trot was easy, and Kara thought of nothing other than how wonderful this was. If only the girls could see her now!

"Good," Bernadette called to her. "Now pick up a canter."

But when Kara asked for the canter, Sally tossed her head and kicked out. Then she jumped up in the air and Kara almost lost her seat.

"Keep going! Don't let her do that to you!" Bernadette yelled. "Do not stop! Keep her moving forward!

Lighten up your hands and keep moving!"

"Trust her, Kara," Bernadette said. "Trust her and just keep moving."

Kara's mind went blank. Bernadette said to trust her. Could she trust Sally? Yes, she could. And she would.

Her heart was beating like a drum, but she was strong and more determined than ever. She loved Sally, and if she didn't do as she was told, everything could fall apart. Sally would be gone.

Soon, Sally relaxed again and cantered around the ring in a nice and easy rhythm. Kara was in heaven. She didn't think about the girls, or her grandfather's barn, or how life used to be. She was riding Sally! Wonderful, beautiful Sally!

When the ride was over and she dismounted, she kissed Sally on the cheek, and couldn't stop talking about every part of the ride.

"I could feel when she was tense, so I kept my hands from grabbing her," she told Bernadette. "She liked me riding her, don't you think? Did you see how I kept my heels down? I think Sally loves me. She's perfect, she's just perfect, there's nothing wrong with Sally!"

Bernadette told her how well she rode. "You did

good, Kara. You did really great. You must be very special because yes, I do believe Sally loves you…"

Kara walked Sally to her stall. "You and me, Sally. That's how it's going to be," she whispered.

Sally was happy too. With Kara riding her, she knew she wouldn't get yelled at or hit. Kara tugged at Sally's mouth sometimes when she was riding, but she was steady enough in her seat. She was like Bernadette, but different. There was something about Kara, and it was good.

As the weeks went by, Kara rode Sally in the ring every day she came to work. At the beginning, Bernadette stayed in the ring and gave them a lesson. But eventually, when Bernadette was busy, Kara got to ride without supervision. Those were the best! Sometimes they just walked and trotted. Sometimes they cantered. And the more Sally was ridden, the happier and calmer she became.

After their ride, Kara would take Sally out on a lead line, and let her eat the grass and weeds that grew up around the barn. This was a lot different than Iowa, and at first, Sally put her nose up in the air. Eat weeds? But she liked being outside with Kara. So eventually, she started putting her nose down to the ground and found a few blades of grass to chew on.

Chapter Seven

One Thursday afternoon, Kara arrived at the barn and before even stopping to say hello to Sally, she looked for Bernadette, who was doing paperwork in the tack room.

Bernadette looked up from the table; she could tell that something was on Kara's mind. "What?" she asked.

Kara was planning to ease into the conversation slowly, but instead, she just blurted it out. "I want to take Sally out on the trail!"

Bernadette looked at Kara and was quiet.

"I can do it. I really can. I understand her now, and I trust her, just like you said I should."

"Kara, it's more complicated than that. The horse has learned that if she bucks at the expressway, she doesn't have to cross it. This is now something she has to unlearn, and it's too dangerous."

"Please, Bernadette. *Please.* I know I can do it. She loves me."

Bernadette was quiet. "Let me think about it, okay?"

"Okay," Kara said. "But just think — if we can get her to cross the road without bucking, maybe she can... earn her keep better."

Bernadette started laughing but then became very serious. "Kara, you've done a great job with her. But she's a high-spirited horse and I'm not so sure the expressway, or city life, is going to work for her. You know because you grew up with horses. You can't make a horse into something that she's not."

This wasn't what Kara wanted to hear, and her heart sank. Bernadette was still thinking of selling Sally? After they had some so far? Now she wished with all her heart she had never brought up the topic of the trails.

She stood still, staring at Bernadette. "Please Bernadette," she said. And her eyes started to tear up, "She loves me. I know she does."

"Kara... it takes more than love. You know that," Bernadette said.

Kara had been around horses long enough to know that Bernadette was right. But still, she could do this. She *had* to do this.

"Bernadette," she said, "We had a horse on the farm that hated to cross a stream. But we taught him to do it. I was with my father, and I got off the horse twice and led him across. My boots got all wet but I didn't care. And the horse got used to it. And then he crossed while I was riding him…"

"A stream is a lot different than a big expressway with cars and trucks whizzing by. But okay. We'll think about it…"

"Okay," Kara said. She was so upset she could barely talk anymore.

As she walked out the door, Bernadette yelled after her, "Kara! *IF* we do this, and it's a big *if* – you'll have to lunge her first. You're also going to have to wear spurs, bring a crop with you, and wear a protective vest."

Kara was so happy she almost shouted out loud. Instead, she whipped around, ran back into the tack room and hugged Bernadette. "You won't be sorry! I promise, I promise! Oh, thank you, THANK YOU!"

Bernadette laughed, "I didn't promise you

anything. I said I'd think about it."

But Kara knew that one day she was going to take her horse out on the trails.

Chapter Eight

It happened only two days later. Kara arrived at the barn early Saturday morning and started to muck out the stalls.

Bernadette walked up to her as she was cleaning Sally's water bucket.

"Okay," Bernadette said. "You want to take that crazy horse out on the trails? You better get her cleaned and tacked, then meet me in the ring. We're going to lunge her but good. And you better keep your legs on her and keep those heels down! Because you're in for a crazy ride, no matter how much she loves you."

Kara couldn't believe what she was hearing.

"This is so great!" Kara yelled after her. "You won't be sorry. I promise!"

She led Sally out of her stall and cleaned her up.

Sally nudged her to see if there were any treats in the pockets of her jacket.

"Okay Sally, this is our big day. Please be good, we have a lot riding on this."

Kara curried and brushed her so that her coat shined like a new penny. She carefully combed out Sally's mane and tail and added conditioner so there wasn't a single tangle. She lifted each leg and picked out her hoofs, talking to her the whole time. When done, she took a damp cloth and wiped her down to get every inch of hay dust and dirt off her body. She wiped Sally's face and kissed the softest part of her nuzzle.

Sally loved the attention, and nickered.

Kara didn't have money to buy new things for Sally, but she did have one special saddle pad that her mother gave her on her birthday. She hardly ever used it because she didn't want it to get dirty or stained, but she took it out for today's celebratory ride. It was a beautiful, quilted brown pad with the words "Cotton Candy Sally" embroidered in orange script on the side. So when they walked down the street, everyone would know Sally's name — and know how extraordinary she was.

"Okay," she called to Bernadette. "We're in the ring!"

Bernadette taught Kara how to lunge Sally, so when Bernadette joined them, Kara started their workout. Sally walked out to the end of the lunge rope, and as soon as Kara told her what to do, she walked in a circle. Soon afterward, they picked up a nice trot – no problems. At the canter, Sally swung her head back and forth and hopped in the air with excitement. But this didn't concern Kara or Bernadette, this was how Sally started every canter when she was on the lunge line. She was just happy.

Bernadette told her, "When we go outside, you're not going to let her swing her head like that. Just remember – outside it's all business."

"I know, "Kara replied. "I promise. I won't let her get away from me."

"Keep her working on the lunge," Bernadette said. "You're going to want her tired before we go outside."

For another ten minutes, they alternated between trot and canter, until Sally had a thin film of sweat on her sides, and was relaxed.

"Okay, I think she's about ready. Get your vest, put her bridle on, and wait here. I'm going to get Joey, and we'll go out. God help us," Bernadette said.

Joey was Bernadette's horse, an unflappable

chestnut thoroughbred who Bernadette took to shows. He did a little bit of everything; dressage, stadium jumping, even cross country when they visited other farms outside of the city. He was kind and patient, and Kara knew he would be a good babysitter for Sally.

Kara could hardly contain herself. There was only one thing in the world that mattered right then, and it was riding the trails on her beautiful Sally.

A few minutes later, Bernadette brought Joey into the ring and got on. "Okay, here we go!" she announced, and outside they went.

They walked towards the park, hugging the side of the road. So far so good. Bernadette made small talk at the beginning, but when the first car passed and Sally jumped, Bernadette told her, "Breathe. Don't forget to breathe. Keep your heels down. Okay, now tell me what you're studying in school…"

Kara knew exactly what Bernadette was doing. Her father used to do the same thing whenever Kara got nervous on a horse. As soon as he saw her tense up, he tried to get her talking about anything and everything else to keep her mind on other things, and keep her breathing.

All she knew was that she couldn't fall off. If she

did, everything would be ruined.

But the closer they got to the expressway, the more anxious Sally became. She looked at everything around her with trepidation, and she spooked every five minutes – jumping up in the air and then bracing her front legs hard when she landed. Her fright and flight instinct was keen, and she was ready to bolt if anything scary appeared or moved suddenly. She hated the city roads! One time she jumped so suddenly and so far to the right that Kara almost lost her stirrups. Her heart was pounding a mile a minute. Maybe this wasn't such a good idea…

Meanwhile, Bernadette kept talking about school and the barn.

When they turned on Lark Street, Sally was already jogging in place and full of tense energy, looking for any opportunity to run home.

Bernadette said firmly "Now listen to me, and listen good. If there's traffic, we'll have to wait until it's clear before we cross. That's when she'll go up in the air, when you make her wait. She won't want to stand still and she won't want to cross. But you're going to keep your legs on her, you're not going to pull on the reins. And you're going to breathe."

"Okay?" she asked.

Kara was holding her breath but managed to get one word out. "Okay," she answered.

It couldn't have gone any worse. As soon as they got close enough to see the traffic, Sally jumped up in the air, turned around and tried to gallop back to the barn. Kara turned her around to face the road, but Sally wasn't having any part it, and when she jumped up in the air for the second time, Kara's foot came out of her left stirrup.

"Whoa!" Bernadette yelled. *"Stop and breathe. NOW! And get your foot back into that stirrup!"*

"I'm trying, but I can't!" Kara answered. "Sally, *STOP!*"

"Whoa Sally!" She cried, and pulled back on the reins. That's when Sally reared and stood up high on her hind legs.

She loved Kara, but this was too much to ask. She was overcome with fright.

Bernadette rode up along the side of her, but now Joey was getting nervous too, and he started to rear. But Bernadette was such a good rider that it didn't phase her. *"Breathe!"* she yelled to Kara. "Stop choking her! Put your leg on that horse and get those heels down. Move her forward!"

She was yelling so many things at once that Kara didn't know what to do first.

"Let her walk, but walk in a circle. You're choking her with the reins! Let your hands go!"

They stood off to the side of the road, and finally, Sally stopped trying to run away. Kara noticed the sweat all over Sally's bridle, and she could feel the horse's heart pounding against her leg. She took a deep breath.

"I don't know what's wrong with her!" Kara shouted.

"She's a horse!" Bernadette said, "And she's scared out of her mind. Take another breath. Pet her and let her know she's okay."

They stood for a minute and Kara put her hand on Sally's neck. She took a deep breath, and just when Sally finally calmed down, Bernadette said they had to start towards the expressway again.

Things went well for a few steps, but then it all fell apart. Sally still wasn't going to get near the whizzing cars, and when Kara pushed her leg against the horse to tell her to move forward, Sally suddenly snorted loudly, stood up on her hind legs, and twisted her body in what felt like three different directions at once. Kara heard Bernadette yelling something, and yelling a lot, but it all happened so fast that she couldn't make out what Bernadette was saying.

Before Kara knew it, she was on the ground.

"OH Sally!" she cried from the pavement. And she grabbed onto the reins that were hanging loose toward the ground.

Bernadette could see that Kara wasn't hurt, and she was proud that the first thing Kara did was grab the reins to make sure Sally wouldn't run home in a frantic, frightened gallop.

"Well," Bernadette said. "At least she didn't run back to the barn. That's an improvement..."

"Ugh," Kara said as she got up. *"SALLY, I'm so mad at you!"* she yelled and groaned at the same time. "I can't believe she did this to me..."

Kara went over to a rock at the side of the road and hoisted herself back on the horse.

"You can be mad at her all you want, Kara. But you didn't help her out. She needed you to be firm and confident. She needed you to be a good rider."

They stood there for a minute to collect themselves, and Kara knew that Bernadette was right. Poor Sally just wasn't in Iowa anymore. She was in New York City, in front of a busy, scary expressway.

Bernadette looked towards the road and saw a clearing through the cars. "We're going to cross Kara. You good?" she asked.

Kara was shocked — they were really going to try this again? Before she knew how she wanted to answer, she blurted out, "Yes, I'm good!"

She could do this. She *WOULD* do this!

"Keep Sally's head right at Joey's tail. Keep her tight up with us, that's going to give her confidence. And we're going to trot across the road as soon as I say so. Nice and easy – and fast!"

"Okay," Kara said.

"You ready?"

"YES!"

In an instant, Bernadette hollered, "*Stay with me!*" and off she went across the road. Kara firmly pressed her legs against Sally's sides, gave the horse her head, and they followed close behind. Sally tried to turn around, but Kara kept her moving forward right at Joey's tail. They were doing it! They were crossing the road!

They kept the trot going until they were well into

the park and could no longer hear the noise of the expressway. Then they walked. The farther they got from the road, the calmer Sally became.

"You okay?" Bernadette said.

"I'm good," Kara replied.

"It was hairy, but you did good Kara. Once you put your mind to it."

"Thanks. I think she's happy now, Bernadette. Look at her! She's relaxed, and her ears are forward!"

"Great, then let's trot and canter."

For the next hour, Sally followed Joey at the walk, trot and canter – and they never took a bad step. Not once did Sally throw her head or spook at anything. As they cantered along the trails in the park, Kara felt free and easy, without a care in the world. And she knew that this was meant to be. They were a real team – just her and Sally. Her father and grandfather used to talk about that feeling all the time. That special bond that only some people found, with some horses. And Kara had that in Sally. They had crossed the road together!

And in her own way, Sally found that special bond with Kara too. Kara cared for her and gave her treats. Every day when no one was looking, she unlatched the chain that kept her head tied to the wall. Kara talked to her, and she could feel the love that Kara had for her. But there was something even more than that. It was that unseen, unexplainable connection that Kara's grandfather had talked about. That's why she whinnied when she heard Kara in the barn. It's why she nudged Kara when she brushed her neck and stood still when Kara picked out her feet. She had found a person again, her person, and it made even New York City feel a little bit like home.

On their way back to the barn, Bernadette told her not to worry about crossing the expressway. She explained that Sally would be much more likely to buck or spook when they were going out, but most horses were more relaxed when on their way home, and that the fastest way to get there was to behave.

She was right. Luckily they didn't have to wait long before the expressway was clear to cross, and while Sally did shy a little in the middle of the road, Kara kept her leg on, and they avoided any kind of a scene. Once they crossed, Kara leaned her head down and hugged Sally's neck, and told her what a wonderful, brave, beautiful horse she was.

***

When they got back to the barn, after Kara had put Sally away and after all the students left, Bernadette asked her to come into the tack room.

"You did really well today Kara, I'm so proud of you."

"Thank you, thank you!" She said. "And I'm so proud of Sally!"

"I know you really love her…"

Something bad was coming, Kara could sense it from the look in Bernadette's face and the tone of her voice.

"*What? What are you going to tell me?*" She cried. "She did great today! She crossed the road! It was hard for her, but she did it. She did it for me. She was happy!"

"No Kara," Bernadette said. "Sally is not happy. And I think you know that."

Kara felt her face turn warm, and as hard as she tried not to cry, her eyes filled up fast with tears.

"She does love you. And you make life bearable for her here. But you know this as well as I do. The city is no place for a horse like her," Bernadette said.

"No, please," Kara cried. "Please don't send her away."

"Kara, look at me," Bernadette said.

Kara sat on the floor and put her head in her hands.

"We're not going to do it right away. I promise you that. I just want you to get ready."

"No, please. I love her. You don't understand. *I have nothing except Sally!*"

Kara was crying so hard she was choking on her words, and it was hard for her to catch her breath.

"Kara…"

"I don't have my father anymore, or anything! Oh please Bernadette," she sobbed. "You don't understand. I can make Sally like it here. I can make her safe for people to ride her…"

"You're a wonderful team. Anybody could see that. But she needs to be in the country. It's not fair to make her cross that expressway and live in the city. She's not that kind of a horse," Bernadette said.

Kara didn't answer. Deep down, she knew Bernadette was right. But how could right feel this wrong?

Kara's sobbing subsided a little bit, and in a small voice she pleaded, "Please… I can make Sally like it here. I'll take extra special care of her…"

"You know horses better than that. Loving you isn't

ever going to make her like that chain that keeps her head to the wall. Or ever make her like eating the weeds that grow around the barn."

"Hey," Bernadette said. "We still have a long way to go before we sell her to a good home. And you're going to help me, okay? And wherever she goes, you'll get visiting rights. Okay?"

Kara tried to catch her breath and stop crying.

"Okay," Kara answered. But when she walked out of the tack room and into Sally's stall, she hugged Sally and cried for a very long time, until the side of Sally's shoulder was wet.

***

That evening over dinner, Kara told her mother everything.

"Oh Kara," she said. "Bernadette's right. New York City is no place for a horse to live…"

"You helped Sally, and she helped you," her mom continued. "Now it's time to let her go. And really, the timing couldn't be better. Because guess what I found out today? Grandpa is going back to the farm."

"What?" Kara asked in surprise. "I thought he sold it…?"

"He did, but he sold it to a "gentleman farmer." That means the owner doesn't work the farm, he and his family just live there on the weekends. They work in Manhattan during the week, and they want Grandpa to help them take care of the farm when they're not there. When Sally gets sold, you can help Grandpa…"

"MOM!" she cried. "We can bring Sally to the farm!"

"Absolutely not," her mother replied. "First of all, Grandpa works there, he doesn't own it anymore. And he's there to take care of the owner's animals, not bring his own. Plus, do you have any idea how much a horse like Sally would cost? She's way out of our league."

"What do you mean?" Kara asked.

"Bernadette never told you about her history?"

"Just that she lived in Iowa, on a farm…."

"She's a very well-bred quarter horse. When she was young, she won a lot of halter classes. When she was older, she won blue ribbons in hunters – all the time. Kara, she was very well known in Iowa…"

"So how did she end up here?" Kara asked.

"Her owner fell on hard times and put her up for sale. Bernadette found out about her and thought she would be a good addition to her barn, for more experienced riders who were ready for a higher level school horse. She spent a lot of money to buy her, thinking it would bring her a new level of clientele. Kids that could go into classes with high fences... and win."

"Mom, I have to buy her. Please. I'll work and raise the money. I can do it."

"She's going to cost thousands of dollars, Kara. You can't do it. And Grandpa can't board her at the barn for free. Be reasonable, please."

"Mom! This isn't fair!"

"Oh Kara, please. I know you love her, but you'll love the animals at Grandpa's too. They have sheep and a miniature donkey..."

"A miniature donkey?" Kara asked sarcastically. "Really, mom? You think I can go from Sally to a miniature donkey?"

Her mother was getting frustrated. "Honey," she said, "I am really tired. I can't have this conversation all night. I'm sorry, but life is not always fair. Be realistic..."

Kara raised her voice. "You know what Mom? I *AM* realistic!" She could hardly catch her breath, and through all her tears, everything just came tumbling out.

"I'm tired of being realistic mom! Daddy's gone. The farm is gone. Everything is gone. All I'm asking for Sally. Why can't I just have one single thing? *Why?*"

She couldn't stop crying, and put her head in her hands, sobbing.

"Kara…" her mother said, and walked over to her.

"Leave me alone!" she cried, and ran out of the kitchen and into her bedroom.

Chapter Nine

It took her awhile, but Kara slowly came to realize that she was never going to own Sally. That's just how it was going to be. She moped around the house and moped around the barn. She even thought about telling her mother and Bernadette she didn't want to go to the barn anymore, but when it came right down to it, she couldn't stay away.

Nobody said another word about selling Sally, at least not in front of her. But Kara knew that people didn't typically buy horses in winter, and it was late November. As Spring approached, it was inevitable. The good thing, she thought, was that Bernadette said she could meet the new owners. Maybe she could work at their barn instead of Bernadette's. Maybe they would even let her ride Sally sometimes. She knew it was wishful thinking, but the longer time went on, the less real it seemed that Sally would be going away.

She took special care now to spend as much time as she could with the mare. Before tacking her up, Kara would curry and brush her until her coat shined. She put polish on her hoofs, and conditioner in her mane and tail. If Sally really was a fancy horse with a special pedigree, Kara was going to make her look that way. Sally let her clip her whiskers, ears, and the hair that grew over her hoofs. Even the girls at the barn started to notice, and they would ask Kara how she made the horse look so fancy.

Kara explained how she did it, and even showed them how to braid Sally's tail and mane. She stood on a little stool so that she was at the right height to reach Sally's mane, and she let them practice making little braids, tucking them under, and then securing each braid with a little black rubber band. Sally looked beautiful! And she loved all the attention and treats the girls gave her.

But the best part was the riding. They never rode out into the park again, but Bernadette taught Kara how to ride Sally low and loose in the ring, like a real hunter. Soon, Bernadette even put up cross rails and showed Kara how to jump the horse. Sally loved to jump, and the rails gave her something to concentrate on instead of bucking. Then they started to jump little fences. Sally got excited and swung her head before each fence, but Kara's legs were strong now, and her riding had improved. So if it ever felt like Sally was going to buck, Kara had her firmly in hand and over the fence they would go.

Kara had to remind herself every now and then that Sally would be sold. But she pushed it out of her mind. If she had a bad day, and couldn't let it go, she would walk into Sally's stall, unlatch the chain, and tell Sally that wherever she went, deep down — she would always be Kara's horse. It was a secret that the two of them shared. Somebody else might pay for her, but Kara and Sally would always belong to one another. No matter what.

Chapter Ten

Every December, Bernadette had a holiday party. But it wasn't the kind of party most people imagine. It was for the horses. Every horse got a red Christmas stocking with their names written on the top with glitter. The stockings were hung next to each horse's stall, and over the course of the week leading up to the party, people would fill the stockings with sugar, peppermints, carrots, and other things that horses loved.

Truly, though, the best part was the tree. They didn't decorate it with tinsel and trinkets like most Christmas trees. Instead, they hung carrots and biscuits. They stuck the candy tight in between the branches, and then one by one, the students took the horses out of their stalls, led them up to the tree, and let them grab the treats they liked. Some horses were shy when they first approached, but most grabbed as many goodies as they could, almost knocking down the whole tree. Everybody laughed and took pictures, and it was great fun for the whole barn.

Kara filled Sally's stocking with more treats every time she came to the barn. But it didn't take long before she noticed that somebody else was filling Sally's stocking, too. She didn't think much about it until two days before the party when it suddenly occurred to her that someone other than Kara was considering Sally as "special." Nobody said anything about new owners, but what if they had been coming to see Sally when she wasn't there? What if they fell in love with her just like Kara had? What if Sally had an interested buyer and nobody told her?

She asked Bernadette about the stocking, but Bernadette was always in such a rush, and never gave Kara a straight answer. She asked other people at the barn too, but they all said they didn't know anything about an owner. In fact, everyone seemed to run away from Kara when she asked, and that started making her very, very nervous.

Kara asked her mother about it too. Her mom had

the same response as everyone else. She said she didn't know of any prospective buyer for the horse, so Kara should just stop worrying.

She tried to stop thinking about it, but it was weighing heavier and heavier on her mind. Especially because the gifts didn't stop. Sally's Christmas stocking was now so full that it started to rip at the sides. And she had a lot more in there than any other horse.

***

Finally, it was the day of the party. Kara was excited to bring Sally to the tree, but she was also worried. Would the new owner be there? Maybe this was Bernadette's way of introducing them? She promised herself she wouldn't cry if that happened. She would be strong and do the right thing – and then when everyone left, only when everyone left, she would go into Sally's stall and talk to her. That's what she would do. But... maybe all the extra gifts were just from Bernadette. Maybe there was no new owner. Kara wasn't sure what to think anymore.

She arrived at the barn early. Bernadette told her there was no riding today, they had too much work to do around the barn, and she needed Kara's help with the party. So when Kara was done cleaning and visiting with Sally, she went right to work. There were a lot of people coming to the party, so everything had to be scrubbed clean. First, she swept the aisles. Then she had to clean the tack room. She was also in charge of the food, so when people started to arrive, she greeted them, took whatever dishes they brought, put them in the refrigerator in the tack room, and made sure everything stayed neat.

When early afternoon came, the barn was so full of people that Kara couldn't keep track of who was there. There were students and their parents, horse owners from other barns, neighbors, workers, parents – they all filled the barn with talking and laughing and wishing happy holidays. Students brought their parents over to see their horses, people were mingling in the aisle, presents started piling up all over the tack room, and soon — there was too much food to fit in the refrigerator. Plus, Bernadette kept giving her new chores to do, so it was impossible for Kara to keep an eye on Sally's stall to see if the new buyer showed up.

After everyone arrived and settled down, it was time for the Christmas tree! It was Kara's job to hold the tree steady as the students brought their horses over, so

Sally would be the last horse to go. This meant that most of the treats would already be eaten, but Kara had a plan: she hid fresh carrots in the tack room, and at the last minute she planned to stick them into the tree for Sally.

One by one people came with their horses to the tree. First the quarter horses approached, and they grabbed at the treats so hard it was all Kara could do to keep the tree upright. Then came the thoroughbreds. They looked so beautiful, and a few of them jumped from the flash of the cameras. Everybody laughed and cheered. Then the Standardbred came down all the aisle, lifting his legs up high in excitement. After that, the school horses and ponies walked down the aisle, and they got the most applause of all. Especially Solomon, who was so big it looked like he wanted to eat the whole tree.

In time, the crowd around the tree got smaller and smaller. Kara was afraid nobody would be left to watch Sally and take their picture, but she saw that Bernadette was nearby, and that was enough for her.

"Okay Kara," Bernadette said at last. "Go get your horse and bring her to the tree…"

Finally! Kara ran down the aisle. But when she

turned the corner in her approach to Sally's stall, she stopped short. Everybody was there, surrounding her horse.

"Come get her, come get your horse!" Jessica yelled to her.

"Yeah, bring Sally to the Christmas tree!" said Susan.

Then she saw her mother by the side of the stall and she panicked. "What's going on? Why are you all here? *What's wrong?*" she cried.

"Just come and bring your horse to the tree already!" someone said.

Kara walked through all the people. Sally's head was at the back of the stall where the chain was, so the only part of her horse that was visible was her tail, which was now meticulously braided, and had red ribbons in it.

"What's going on?" she said again as she walked into the stall. Someone had also braided her mane and twisted red ribbons in it. Sally nickered as Kara hugged her, and Kara gave her a biscuit that was in her pocket.

"Read the card!" Susan yelled, and then everybody started chanting the same thing, *"Read the card... read the card!"*

Kara didn't know what to think. But she did as she was told, and removed the envelope that was taped to the wall above Sally's feed bucket. Then she opened the card:

Dear Kara,

Sometimes bad things happen to good people and to good horses. But sometimes good things happen, too. You will always be my person, and I will always be your horse. Life is full of surprises. So surprise! Please take good care of me. I love you. Merry Christmas to you, my special person.

Love, Sally (and Bernadette)

Kara turned around to look at Bernadette, who had walked into the stall behind her.

"She's yours," Bernadette said softly. "She was yours ever since you first met her. Now, it's official."

Kara did the one thing she promised herself she wouldn't do; the tears filled up in her eyes and she said, "I don't understand…"

Everybody started laughing.

"You own Sally now, and she owns you, Kara.

Merry Christmas…"

Kara put her head in her hands. She tried so hard, but she couldn't stop the tears from flowing. She put her arms around her horse, and it was only then that she realized someone had unlatched Sally's chain. Sally nudged her and sniffed around for other treats that might be in her pocket.

Kara felt numb. Could this really be happening? How? And why? She barely noticed that all eyes were on her and Sally. She barely noticed all the picture taking. And all the talking and commotion. Until finally, someone called out, "bring her to the tree! Bring Sally to the tree!"

Kara took her lead line and backed Sally out of the stall, just like she had done hundreds of times. But now it felt different. This was *her* horse, *Sally was hers!* Everybody stood to the side as they walked down the aisle, turned the corner and approached the tree. Sally looked spectacular in all her shine and glitter, and walked calmly next to Kara as they approached the tree. Someone had decorated it with fresh biscuits and carrots, and Sally ate them all.

***

When the barn was quiet, and everyone had left, Bernadette, Kara, and her mother sat in the tack room and Bernadette explained...

"Is this real? Really real?" Kara asked.

"As real as real can be," Bernadette said.

"But how? I thought Sally was so expensive. And will we keep her here? What about the owner?"

"There never was another owner. Everybody at the barn knew what was going to happen, and they wanted to give you and Sally special presents," her mother said. "That's why all those treats mysteriously appeared in her stocking."

Do you know what *paying it forward* means?" Bernadette asked her.

"No," Kara said. "And what does it have to do with Sally and me?"

"A long time ago, someone did a wonderful thing for me. They gave me a chance when I thought there was none. That's how I got his barn, Kara. Someone believed in me, and gave me a gift without ever wanting anything in return."

"*Paying it forward* means you take the good that someone did for you once, and then give good to someone else. You pay the good fortune forward."

Kara listened closely.

"You and Sally. All I could say is that it makes me feel good to keep you together. You're a team and you'll help each other – just as you always have. But one day," Bernadette continued, "You need to pay this goodness forward, and do something good for someone else. That's how it works."

"There's something else," her mother interrupted. "New York City is not the place for her. So she's moving to Grandpa's farm."

"I thought the gentleman farmer didn't want her?" Kara exclaimed.

"He's going to take her, so long as you help Grandpa with the farm. You're going to have to muck out stalls and pick manure out of the pastures. You're going to have to clean the tack room and help Grandpa take care of the donkey and the sheep."

"I can do that! I would love to do that!" Kara cried.

"It's all going to happen very fast," Bernadette said, "Because the trailer is coming tomorrow morning to pick her up. This way you can spend a full week with her at her new home, and get her settled in before you go back to school."

Kara was overwhelmed. She suddenly realized how

much she loved Bernadette, and that she would miss her terribly. She started to cry.

"I'm not crying from being sad! I promise!"

"Well," Bernadette said. "Don't think you're getting rid of me so fast. I'm coming to visit the farm next weekend to check up on you both. It's only an hour away, so don't think you're getting rid of me so fast!"

Kara walked over to Bernadette. "I love you," she cried. *"Thank you so much...."*

***

Kara arrived at Bernadette's barn early the next morning and went straight into Sally's stall.

"I'm taking this chain off for the last time, Sally. I love you, and this is just the beginning of new adventures for you and me... forever!"

She put Sally on the cross ties and cleaned her up better than ever before. She put shipping boots on her legs, and put on a special halter with sheep skin so Sally wouldn't get rubs on her face. Then she went out to the trailer to make sure everything was in good form, and that the hay bag was full.

Her mother and Bernadette watched as Sally and

Kara walked together, out of the barn and up to the trailer. Beautiful, sassy, shiny Sally walked up the ramp and right into the trailer without a balk or a buck. She had a very good feeling about things to come.

###

ABOUT THE AUTHOR

KAREN BELOVE discovered the magic of horses long ago, while mucking out stalls at a riding school in New York City. That's where she bought her first horse, and when her horse adventures began. Since then, she has been involved in many aspects of the sport, including dressage, eventing, and cross-country jumping.

Ms. Belove thought about writing *The Sally Horse Chronicles* when she first fell in love with horses at that riding school in New York — and has now made the series a reality. She still spends much of her time in New York City, but has a home in upstate New York where she rides the beautiful horse trails of Dutchess County. Ms. Belove also has a golden retriever and four cats, all of whom love horses almost as much as she does.

DON'T MISS THE NEXT HEARTFELT BOOK IN THE *SALLY HORSE CHRONICLES #2*

COTTON CANDY SALLY MEETS A FRIEND

Sally moves out of New York City and loves her new life among the trees and green grass of Long Island. She's so happy that she starts winning blue ribbons at hunter shows, and people are calling her "lovely" and "special" instead of "nasty" and "sour."

But something strange happens when they arrive at the second show of the season. Sally jumped the first fence beautifully — but when she rode along the long side of the field, past other horses and spectators — she suddenly bucked, threw her head up and whinnied loudly in the middle of her class. Kara couldn't get her settled, and they crashed into fence #2. Was something hurting her? Why was she becoming frightened and uncooperative, like she was at Bernadette's riding school? Kara was baffled and worried — what was Sally trying to tell her?

CPSIA information can be obtained at www.ICGtesting.com
Printed in the USA
LVOW07s2306110916

504188LV00001B/23/P